The Legend of the White Doe

William H. Hooks

Illustrated by Dennis Nolan

Tom Lanning

Macmillan Publishing Company   New York

For B.A.H., Jr.,

better known as Buddy

Macmillan Publishing Company, 866 Third Avenue, New York, NY 10022
Collier Macmillan Canada, Inc.
Printed and bound in Japan

First American Edition   10 9 8 7 6 5 4 3 2 1

The text of this book is set in 14 point Perpetua. The illustrations are rendered in watercolor.
Library of Congress Cataloging-in-Publication Data
Hooks, William H.   The legend of the white doe.
Summary: After the English colony on Roanoke Island is attacked by hostile Indians, the survivors
live with a friendly tribe, and Virginia Dare finds her first love coming to a tragic and
supernatural end. 1. Dare, Virginia, b. 1587—Juvenile fiction. 2. Raleigh's Roanoke colonies,
1584–1590—Juvenile fiction. 3. Indians of North America—Juvenile fiction. [1. Dare, Virginia, b.
1587—Fiction. 2. Roanoke Island (N.C.)—History—Fiction. 3. Raleigh's Roanoke colonies,
1584–1590—Fiction. 4. Indians of North America—Fiction] I. Nolan, Dennis, ill. II. Title.
PZ7.H7664Le   1988   [Fic]   87-11176   ISBN 0-02-744350-7

Contents

The True Story

In 1587, Sir Walter Raleigh established a colony of English men, women, and boys in the New World, on Roanoke Island. Before his ships left the New World for the return to England, one of the colonists gave birth to a child, the first English child born in America. She was named Virginia Dare.

Two Indians, Manteo and Wanchese, had gone to England a year before with a party of English explorers. They had learned the language and had returned to the New World with the colonists.

The colonists were promised supply ships within a year. But three years passed before Sir Walter Raleigh was able to send provisions to them. When the supply ships finally reached Roanoke Island, they found the colony deserted and the word CROATOAN carved on a post. The rescuers assumed that the colonists had moved to the island of Croatoan to be safe with their Indian friend Manteo. Tropical storms prevented their sailing to Croatoan Island. The search was abandoned, and the colonists were never found.

Many legends about the colonists abound in the area where they disappeared. One that their English and Indian descendants still tell today—four hundred years later—is the legend of the white doe. This is the way they tell it.

Savages in London Towne

In the depths of the wild, mysterious Great Dismal Swamp there roams a ghost deer. A night creature, shining in the moonlight, shimmering like a silvery phantom, the white doe is none other than the living spirit of Ulalee. Ulalee, the beautiful adopted daughter of Chief Manteo. But Ulalee's story begins far, far from these shores. It begins in London Towne.

Long ago a great boat with white wings, carrying strange men with pale skins and hair the color of corn silk, came to our shores. They gave us red cloth and shiny tin cups. We gave them pearls and smoking tobacco. We feasted the strangers in our homes and went as guests aboard their great winged boat. We delighted in their company and they in ours. When it was time for the strangers to return to their land, the Sea Captain invited some of our men to go with them. Chief Manteo and Wanchese felt honored to be chosen to see the wonders of the kingdom beyond the waters of the endless sea.

After many weeks the boat with white wings came to the end of the endless sea. The Sea Captain steered the boat up a mighty river to a great city called London Towne. The fair-skinned people who dwelt beyond the endless waters had never seen the likes of Manteo and Wanchese. "Savages from the Indies," they called them. And they meant no harm by the use of the word *savage*. Our beginnings were friendly.

The Sea Captain asked Chief Manteo and Wanchese to dress in their best robes and finest jewels. "We'll give these Englishmen a show," he shouted. "We'll make them a parade they will long remember! We'll pop the eyes of all London Towne—even the good Queen Elizabeth herself!"

Now, it seems the Queen must have been expecting wondrous things. She sent pipers and drummers, strong men with sedan chairs, and a Towne Crier to meet the Sea Captain, fresh returned from the New World.

The pipers puffed away, and the drummers rumbled like thunder.

"Manteo and Wanchese, seat yourselves on the sedan chairs!" shouted the Sea Captain.

Chief Manteo and Wanchese stepped forth decked in fine furs and bright feathers, with jewels and gold chains round their necks and pearls like bunches of grapes swinging from their ears. Sailors bearing chests and prize boxes fell in line behind the sedan chairs. The Sea Captain and his officers mounted finely caparisoned horses to lead the parade.

"Clear the way! Make way, make way!" shouted the Towne Crier.

"To the Queen's palace!" roared the Sea Captain. And off they marched through the streets of London Towne, with the curious crowd shouting on every side.

"Savages from the Indies!"

"Heathen chieftains! I'll bet they can cast spells!"

"Look at the gold and pearls! Did you ever see such a sight?"

"What will the good Queen Bess think of all this?"

Just as the people of London Towne were bedazzled by Manteo and Wanchese, they, in turn, were in awe of the great treeless city with its tall buildings, strange people, and foul-smelling streets. They were glad to be riding high in their sedan chairs.

At the palace Manteo and Wanchese were received with honor by Queen Elizabeth. The good Queen stared at the strange bronze men in their feathers and furs and jewels, never having seen such creatures. And Manteo and Wanchese could not take their eyes from the splendid Queen with the chalk-white face and crinkly hair the color of flame.

But the Queen quickly put them at ease. "A banquet is set, my lords, in your honor," she said. "Come, let us feast and celebrate the wonders of the New World."

Although he could speak little of the Queen's language, Chief Manteo seemed to understand all that she said. And the Queen was much pleased with Chief Manteo's gift for talking with his hands. He drew pictures in the air, making the things he wished to say clear to all. But Wanchese sat silent most of the time, seeming awkward and ill at ease with the English court.

At the end of the sumptuous banquet, steaming pitchers of hot tea were brought to the tables.

"Your Majesty, we have prepared a special tea from the New World," announced the Sea Captain.

The Queen sniffed the fragrant brew and asked, "What do you call it?"

"Sassafras!" boomed Chief Manteo.

"Sassafras? What a funny name!" cried the Queen. "Sassafras!" she said again, giggling like a young girl.

"Sassafras! Sassafras!" the lords and ladies echoed.

"Delicious!" said the Queen, taking a sip. "I do hope you brought me lots of sassafras, Chief Manteo."

Chief Manteo smiled and nodded his head, and the Sea Captain replied, "We did indeed, Your Majesty."

After the splendid feast, Chief Manteo took out his long clay pipe. He filled it with tobacco and used a candle to light it. The Queen and all her court watched him intently as he put the pipe in his mouth, puffed away on it, and blew smoke through his nostrils and into the air.

"The savage is on fire!" cried a lady of the court.

Chief Manteo puffed again on his pipe. He blew a circle of smoke into the air and grinned, seeming none the worse for it. Then he handed the Queen the pipe and gestured for her to try it.

The Queen hesitated only a moment. She put the pipe to her mouth and took a noble puff. Her eyes bulged and she coughed and spit, sending clouds of smoke around her head.

"Sir," she said to Chief Manteo, gasping, "this thing bites like a serpent!"

The lords and ladies held their breath, expecting the Queen's temper to flare.

"But I'll master the smoking clay dragon yet," she declared. "What do you feed this monster?" she asked.

"Tobacco," said Chief Manteo.

"We'll try this tobacco another time," said the Queen. "Bring me more of that fine sassafras tea to quench the bite of the tobacco serpent."

Well, that was just the beginning of a long round of entertainments for Chief Manteo and Wanchese. All of London Towne were determined to see and touch the strange plumed savages from the New World. To keep the crowds from crushing them, the Queen sent her own guards with them through the streets.

Chief Manteo loved the curious English people. He beckoned to them and shouted in their own tongue, "Friends! My friends!"

Wanchese remained solemn and cold, seeming to wish only to return to his people as soon as possible.

Meanwhile the Queen gave orders to send a colony of men, women, and boys to the New World. The boats were filled with all the things the colonists would need for the long journey—tools and clothes and foods that would not spoil. They were also stocked with swords and guns and gunpowder. It took a long time to gather the people who dared to cross the endless sea, and to fill the boats with their belongings.

When all was ready, the Queen summoned Manteo and Wanchese. "I have gifts of friendship for you," she said. "Go back to your land with my people, and dwell there in peace together." She gave them each a box wrapped in royal velvet and bid them good-bye.

A huge crowd gathered to see the men, women, and boys sail out of London Towne with Manteo and Wanchese. They shouted and cheered and wished them Godspeed until the boats turned a bend in the river and vanished from sight.

That first night at sea, Chief Manteo and Wanchese opened their gifts from Queen Elizabeth. Manteo's was a garter set with rubies and emeralds. Wanchese's gift was an English arrow hammered from pure silver. Manteo watched Wanchese rub the shaft of the shining arrow with the tips of his fingers. For the first time since their arrival in London Towne, Wanchese smiled.

Friends and Foes

*T*he passage from London Towne to our homeland was a long and trying one. The great winged boats that looked so large were filled to bursting with people and supplies. Within a week, tempers flared and fights broke out. Master John White, whom the Queen had appointed Governor of the colony, was hard put to keep peace.

It is said that the only two people on board who never complained were Chief Manteo and Mistress Elinor Dare. Now, Mistress Dare was the daughter of Governor White. And she was large with child when the journey began. Mistress Dare delighted in teaching Chief Manteo new English words. And Chief Manteo taught her many words from his language. But she liked best learning the hand signs that he showed her. They passed many pleasant hours while the others grumbled about the bad food, the foul water, and the cramped quarters.

Wanchese grew more and more solemn. He would speak to no one except Chief Manteo. He ate little and grew thin. His days were spent in the prow of the boat, looking out over the sea in the direction of his homeland. Each dawn he pulled a small stick from his robe and carved a notch on it to mark the days of the journey.

When Wanchese's time stick had 76 notches carved on it, land was sighted. The English thanked their God, and Chief Manteo and Wanchese made a prayer to the Great Spirit.

The colonists landed on Roanoke Island. With feet on dry land and breathing space for all, everyone's spirits lifted. Friendly Indians brought them fish, deer, and squashes, and joined them in a bountiful feast on the sandy shores of Roanoke.

Everything happened quickly. During the next few weeks, the colonists built daub and wattle houses, which were made of tree branches plastered with clay. Many of Chief Manteo's friends came to help, and soon the colonists were settled in their new homes.

One splendid day Chief Manteo was made Lord of Roanoke. The colonists and a great throng of Manteo's friends gathered for the occasion. Though her baby would be born any day, Mistress Dare insisted on attending the ceremony to witness the honor bestowed upon her friend, Chief Manteo.

"Her Majesty, Queen of England, gave me sealed orders before leaving London," said Governor White. "I was instructed to open the orders only upon arriving safely in the New World. Among them was the command to bestow a title on Chief Manteo."

"A title, sir?" asked Chief Manteo.

"Her Majesty bestows upon one who is already honored in his own country a title given in her country only to men of the highest merit. Her Majesty has ordered me, as her agent, to create the first Lord in the New World. If this title suits you, Chief Manteo, please kneel and I shall do as my Queen instructs."

Chief Manteo solemnly knelt and bowed his head.

Governor White laid the tip of his sword on Chief Manteo's head. "In the name of Her Majesty, I dub thee Lord of Roanoke," he proclaimed. "Rise, Lord Manteo."

Lord Manteo rose and embraced the governor. The hushed crowd broke into thunderous cheers and shouts of "Long live Lord Manteo!"

Wanchese watched the ceremony from the edge of the crowd. His pride was pricked that the Queen had made no mention of him in her sealed orders. He did not come forward to embrace Lord Manteo. And when Lord Manteo went to him, Wanchese turned his back and mumbled darkly, "These people have no right to be here. I'll see that they do not stay."

Lord Manteo touched his shoulder in the gesture of friendship. But Wanchese shook him off angrily and ran swiftly into the nearby woods.

Just four days after Manteo became Lord of Roanoke, Mistress Dare's baby was born.

"It's a girl! A bouncing baby girl!" shouted the midwife from the door of Mistress Dare's house.

"The heavens be praised!" shouted Annais Dare, the baby's father.

"Open the good English port I put by for this occasion!" ordered Governor White, the baby's grandfather.

The air rang with "Hip, hip, hurray!" It's a wonder that Queen Elizabeth herself didn't hear the cheers in London Towne.

"Let my daughter be named Virginia in honor of our Virgin Queen Elizabeth," said Annais Dare. "A toast to Virginia Dare, my daughter, the first English child born in the New World!"

"Hip, hip, hurray!" shouted the English people and the Indians.

Lord Manteo stepped forward and spoke. "Let it be known to all that this child, this Virginia Dare, will always be cherished as though she were a child of my own people. Always she will have our protection. And always she will have our love."

There was more cheering and toasting on that happy day.

After the celebrations, the Sea Captain prepared his boats to sail to London Towne. As the time drew near for the boats to leave, the colonists began to worry. They feared the Sea Captain might not return within a year, as planned. They persuaded Governor White to go with him to England to insure that the supply ships came back. The Governor was reluctant to leave his daughter and granddaughter. "Nothing under heaven shall prevent my return," he declared. He embraced his daughter and kissed the infant, Virginia Dare, and set sail with the winged boats.

The colonists stayed on the beach until the white wings of the boats flapped one last time in the sunlight, then slipped from sight.

Mistress Dare hugged little Virginia close. She was suddenly cold despite the sparkling sun.

Lord Manteo bid the colonists good-bye. "It is time I returned to my family in Croatoan," he said. "I have been away too long and yearn to see them. Should you want for anything, you have but to send a messenger. Croatoan is two days south of here."

In the weeks that followed, a great hush fell over the little colony. Without the Sea Captain and his crew, and without Lord Manteo and his friends, the colonists felt truly alone. They were kept busy preparing their homes for the first winter on Roanoke Island. Although they were lonely, they never felt afraid in the New World—until the night they were awakened by loud cries.

"Fire! Help! Fire! Our house is on fire!"

Flaming arrows rained down on the daub and wattle

houses. The roof of the house nearest the woods burned brightly, lighting up the little village.

A horn was sounded. Three short blasts, followed by a rest, then three more short blasts signaled danger.

The entire village was awakened. Men grabbed their guns and rushed from the houses.

Mistress Dare watched from the doorway as her husband, still in his nightshirt, dashed outside to join the men.

The sound of gunfire and the shouts of the colonists rang in the firelit night. Suddenly a horrendous war cry rent the air as Indians broke from their cover in the woods and attacked. To everyone's surprise, Wanchese was leading the warriors.

The colonists took aim and fired into the onrushing throng. Two Indians dropped. Several more were wounded. None of them, except Wanchese, had ever encountered the firing sticks of the pale men. They showered the colonists with one final round of arrows and fled back into the protective forest.

That shower of arrows was a deadly one. By the first pale light of morning, the colonists counted their losses. Five young men were dead, and another half dozen injured. Mistress Dare's husband, Annais, lay mortally wounded. And the friendship between the English and the Indians was dealt a mighty blow.

A Secret Code

That very day Mistress Dare sent runners south to seek help from Lord Manteo. The men stood guard while the runners made their way to Croatoan.

On the second day the colonists buried their dead as best they could, in shallow sandy graves. Mistress Dare read from the *English Book of Common Prayer,* there being no priest among them. She spoke the words clearly, but with much effort, for her husband was one of those committed to the hands of the English God.

On the morning of the fourth day, the weary runners returned to the little colony with Lord Manteo and a hundred of his finest warriors.

"My faithful friend, it is good to see you," said Mistress Dare. "We fear for our very lives."

"Those are fears we can dispel," said Lord Manteo. "I only wish I had the power to lift the great sorrow of your loss. Blood has stained the friendship between our people and yours."

"How, Lord Manteo, can you make us feel safe again?" asked Mistress Dare.

"I offer you haven with my people. Come with us to Croatoan. You shall want for naught."

"Some of our men are wounded. They are too ill to travel. And I am loathe to leave this place where I expect my father to arrive in the early spring."

Lord Manteo was silent for a minute. "I respect your wishes, Mistress Dare. If you must stay here, my warriors will help you build a stout fort."

"A stout fort. Yes, a fort that will see us safely through the winter. You are a generous man."

The able-bodied colonists and Lord Manteo's warriors set about raising the fort. Tall trees were cut and set firmly into the ground to form a strong and solid wall. The tree trunks were sharpened at the tops to prevent their being scaled. Soon a large, circular wall enclosed the daub and wattle cottages, and a massive front gate of logs joined the ends securely. A small, secret gate was cleverly built into the back of the fort. It was finished— but not before sharp cold morning frosts told the colonists that winter was upon them.

"I must return with my warriors," said Lord Manteo.

"How can we ever thank you, dear friend?" asked Mistress Dare.

"I only wish you could return with me to Croatoan," replied Lord Manteo.

Mistress Dare was silent.

"At least consider coming with little Virginia and the other women and boys. The men can hold the fort until the supply boats come."

"I am sure Governor White is at this very moment preparing the supply ships. I want to be here to greet my father," said Mistress Dare. "And, thanks to you, Lord Manteo, we will be safe behind our stout walls."

Lord Manteo and his warriors left. Again a great lonely silence fell upon the colony. But this time fear also abided in the silence, for the colonists worried that Wanchese might strike again.

The winter was cold and rainy. Food supplies grew dangerously low and what little remained became moldy and tainted. Each day the colonists strained their eyes over the endless waters in the direction of England. But no sail broke upon the emptiness of the sea.

By the time spring came, the colonists were completely out of food. They were depending on fish and whatever game the men could shoot. Hunger brought to the surface the doubts and fears all were having but none had spoken about. First there were whispers. Then public arguments.

"We're abandoned for sure."

"The supply ships must have gone down in a storm."

"They were taken by Spanish pirates."

"We'll starve in this godforsaken land!"

"Starve we will, unless the savages kill us first!"

Then one morning two of the men rushed back from

hunting to report they had sighted strange Indians. This brought matters to a head.

"Surely they are scouts from Wanchese," cried the hunters.

"Let us go now, while we can, to Croatoan," begged the women. "Only Lord Manteo can protect us."

A council was called. It was decided that every man, woman, and boy should have a vote in the decision. Only Mistress Dare voted to stay on in the fort to await the coming of the supply boats. But the colonists would not hear of such a thing. And for the sake of her child, she was persuaded to leave the fort.

"Before we go, there is something we must do. Something that I promised my father, Governor White," said Mistress Dare.

"Whatever it is, let's be swift about it," said one of the hunters.

"I promised my father that if we left this spot, we would carve on a post or a tree the name of the place where we were going."

"I can carve letters with my knife!" cried one of the boys. "Let me carve Croatoan on the gatepost of the fort."

"Wait! We had a code. A secret code between us. I was to carve a cross above the name if we left unwillingly or were taken by enemies. The question is: Do we go freely to friends? Or are we forced to leave by enemies? Which is true?"

"If we go now, and to Lord Manteo, we go freely to friends!" shouted a man.

"If we wait until the scouts report back to Wanchese, it may be another story!" warned the hunters.

"Let us go right now!" urged the women.

"Let us pack and be ready to leave at daybreak," suggested Mistress Dare.

They all agreed that daybreak would be the time to leave.

"Do I carve the cross over the word Croatoan?" asked the boy.

"I think not," said Mistress Dare. "There's no need to worry the Governor about something that may not happen."

By sundown all the colonists had backpacks filled with as much as they could carry. They buried in the courtyard of the fort the things they could not take with them. It had been a long hard day, and all were eager to rest before starting the journey. Guards were posted, and everyone else lay down at first dark.

Just as they began to doze, the guards spotted campfires flickering in the distant woods. Quickly they roused the colonists. And just as quickly it was decided to leave, under cover of darkness, by the small secret gate at the back of the fort.

With a heavy load on her back and little Virginia in her arms, Mistress Dare looked around the fort one last time. Her eye caught the freshly carved word on the gatepost—CROATOAN, spelled out in fine Roman letters. Should she quickly scratch a cross above the word? She hesitated, then turned and hurried through the narrow gate at the back of the fort.

A Haven in Croatoan

The colonists crept to their small boats on the shore and quietly paddled south. They skimmed across the narrow waters to the long string of outer banks that led to Croatoan. Then they beached the boats and hid them under broken tree branches.

All night long they trudged along the sandy ground, moving south, guided by the stars. By daybreak they were exhausted. They stopped to rest, and to take their first look back. In the light of the sun's red rays they saw a towering pillar of black smoke rising from Roanoke. Everyone talked at once.

"There goes our fort!"

"There but for the grace of God we'd be burned alive or shot through with arrows."

"We can rest only a little while."

"It's still more than a day's journey to Lord Manteo."

The black pillar of smoke behind them put fear in their hearts and strength in their legs. They pushed on.

All day they walked south doggedly, with only short rests to ease the weight of the heavy backpacks. By sundown they still had not reached Croatoan, but they were far enough from Roanoke to risk resting the night.

Before dawn they moved south again. And when the sun was sitting in its midday zenith, they stumbled into Lord Manteo's village.

Such a welcome was made for the colonists that they quickly forgot sore backs and aching feet. Lord Manteo's mother, Lady Winona, a woman of great power and wisdom, prepared a bountiful feast to celebrate the coming of their English friends. By nightfall deer and wild pig had been well roasted over turning spits. All manner of fish had been smoked and barbecued. New corn lay steaming in its green husks. And there were melons and berries and a potent drink made from wild grapes.

"This cannot compare with the banquets of your mighty Queen Elizabeth," said Lord Manteo. "But our welcome to you is certainly as great."

"More so, my lord," answered Mistress Dare. "You have rescued us, not once, but twice now. We owe you much."

Lady Winona spoke to Lord Manteo and then nodded toward Mistress Dare.

"My mother wants me to tell you that if you feel in our debt, then she asks a favor."

"Anything. Please tell Lady Winona that I will do anything within my power for her."

Lord Manteo and Lady Winona spoke in their own language.

"My mother requests that you and little Virginia come to stay in her house. That is the favor she asks."

Mistress Dare said yes in the Indian language that she had learned from Lord Manteo. "Tell Lady Winona that I apologize for knowing so little of her language, but it will be a comfort to stay for a few days as her guest."

The colonists feasted long into the evening under the night sky studded with stars. When the moon had made a silvery path on the glass-smooth ocean, a group of young girls appeared on the sandy shores. They were draped in the long gray mosses from the giant water oaks, and they danced and sang like water nymphs.

The colonists felt warm and safe that first enchanted night in Croatoan.

While waiting for cottages to be built for the colonists, Mistress Dare enjoyed the comfort of Lady Winona's house. And Lady Winona doted on little Virginia.

"You'll spoil my babe rotten!" chided Mistress Dare.

But Lady Winona only smiled and said in her own language, "It's impossible to spoil a babe."

Living in Croatoan among Lord Manteo's people was pleasant, but all of the colonists felt it was temporary. Surely the English boats would come before the summer was finished. Surely they would find the word CROATOAN carved on the gatepost of the abandoned fort. Surely then they would sail directly to Lord Manteo's village.

Every day, just before sunset, Mistress Dare would take little Virginia and go alone to the water's edge. There she would stand with the babe in her arms, looking out to sea.

Summer passed. Winter followed. Spring came again. And still no sail appeared on the horizon.

Virginia began to talk, speaking the Indian language as well as the English. Mistress Dare would laugh and tease her. "You're more a child of the Indies than a proper English lass!" she'd say. And so she was, running wild and free with the Indian children.

Five peaceful years passed at Croatoan. Most of the colonists gave up hope of supply ships. Some of the younger men took Indian wives and adopted Indian ways. But during all those years, Mistress Dare never stopped looking for a ship from England. She went to the ocean every day with Virginia. The young child, ordinarily so restless, would hold her mother's hand and stand very still while the two of them kept their faithful vigil.

Then one day as they stood together, staring into the watery vastness, Mistress Dare let out a cry so piercing it brought the Indian women running from their homes.

"A sail! A sail!" she screamed. "There! Out there! An English sail!"

The Indian women rushed down to the sea. "Where? Where?" they asked.

"There! Making for the shore!" shouted Mistress Dare.

The Indian women strained their eyes, scanning the whole horizon. But they saw nothing.

"A ship! An English ship! Father!" cried Mistress Dare.

She began walking into the waves, pulling Virginia along with her. "Father!" she called, pushing farther into the sea.

"Come back!" warned the women. "There's nothing out there!" they shouted to her.

But Mistress Dare moved deeper and deeper into the ocean. Soon she was in water over Virginia's head. A young Indian maid dived into the sea and swam to the mother and child. She grabbed the child and pleaded with Mistress Dare to turn back.

Mistress Dare released Virginia's hand, then plunged forward, crying, "Father, I knew you would come!"

A surging wave carried her under. The Indian maid rode the wake of the same wave back to shore, bringing the half-drowned child with her. Mistress Dare was seen no more.

The women took Virginia to Lady Winona, who nursed her back to health and adopted the child as her own.

Ulalee

*L*ady Winona pondered on an Indian name for Virginia Dare.

"Let me see. What can I call a child who runs like the wind? One whose feet never seem to touch the ground? What can I call a little bird that will never be quite tame? My little bird. That's it! I'll call you Ulalee, after the wood thrush."

"Ulalee! Ulalee!" chanted Virginia, tasting the sound of her new name. She flapped her arms like wings and ran in circles, singing "Ulalee!" until she was dizzy. Then she staggered to Lady Winona and collapsed in her adoptive mother's lap.

So Ulalee grew up in Lady Winona's house. By the time she was fourteen she was the fairest young woman you could picture. She was pale complexioned, with strawberry hair and eyes the color of wild violets. And she did have pleasing ways. True to her name, she sang like the sweetest of birds.

At night the villagers would gather around the fire to

hear Ulalee sing. Lady Winona would sigh and say, "I knew I was right to name her Ulalee, after the wood thrush that sings best among all birds."

Now, in the natural turn of seasons, all the young men—both the English and the Indian—started taking notice of Ulalee. Many came to Lady Winona's house to ask the pleasure of walking by the sea at sunset with Ulalee. She would have naught to do with any of them. Oh, she would laugh and tease them, but never walk alone with any of them. After a time the young men gave up trying. All but one, a young Indian lad named Okisko.

Okisko took Ulalee's teasing. He even teased her back and sometimes made her laugh. Other times he made her angry.

"Stop pestering me!" she cried. "Go hunting with the other braves."

"What shall I bring my Ulalee from the hunt?" asked Okisko.

"Bring me down from a wild goose to make a feather pillow," she snapped.

Okisko returned the next day with three wild geese. "These will make a soft pillow, and maybe warm a cold heart," he said.

Ulalee laughed and said, "Come at sunset. We'll walk by the sea."

Shortly thereafter, Okisko came to Lord Manteo and Lady Winona to ask for Ulalee's hand. He gave the ceremonial greeting, as all young men must on such occasions. Then he presented a large bowl of ripe grapes to Lady Winona and a choice portion of venison to Lord Manteo. Ulalee stood to one side with her head bowed shyly, as was becoming to young maidens.

When Okisko was finished with the traditional greeting, he added a statement of his own in a strong and urgent voice. "I will love and protect Ulalee always, even with my life's blood."

Out of the corner of her eye, Ulalee watched Lady Winona and Lord Manteo. Large tears trickled down Lady Winona's face. Lord Manteo stood silent and solemn, with a frown on his forehead. Ulalee was greatly puzzled.

Finally Lord Manteo spoke. "Nothing would please me more than to see you young people joined." He swallowed hard and continued. "But Ulalee has been spoken for by another." Without further explanation he strode from the house.

Silence like thick ground fog filled the house. Ulalee was the first to speak. "Lord Manteo has told me nothing of this. I don't understand. Never has he kept secrets from me. How could I be spoken for, and my own mother not tell me?"

Lady Winona said nothing. The weight of great sorrow clouded her tear-stained face.

Ulalee began to cry. She hugged Lady Winona and begged her to make Lord Manteo grant Okisko's request.

"Child, child, you know I'd give my wood thrush anything," said Lady Winona. "But this? I cannot be sure. It must be handled most carefully."

At last Okisko was able to ask Lady Winona, "Who has spoken for Ulalee?"

"None other than Cipo," Lady Winona replied, "the most powerful medicine man in Croatoan."

"But he is old and ugly!" screamed Ulalee. "I'd die before I'd marry him. How could you love me and consider such a thing?"

"I'll kill him," declared Okisko.

"Quiet, my young ones," ordered Lady Winona. "The winds may carry your words to Cipo's ears. He hears things without being present. Lord Manteo has done what he can already. He has told Cipo that our Ulalee is too young to marry. He has gained some time, but I don't know how long we can refuse him."

"Then we'll run far from Croatoan and old Cipo," said Ulalee.

"I have friends on the mainland. We could go there," declared Okisko.

"How young and unwise you are, my loves," cried Lady Winona. "You can run from Cipo, but not from his powerful magic. Don't try anything foolish. Be patient. Let Lord Manteo play Cipo along. Time could bring changes." Then she drew the young ones close in her arms and whispered, "Cipo is old. You are young. Be

patient, my wood thrush."

Now, that was good advice from a wise lady. But patience is something better practiced by the old than the young. Okisko and Ulalee walked by the sea at sunset and made plans to leave Croatoan. They were foolish enough to believe that the roar of the sea and the slap of the waves breaking on the sands would hide their secret.

"We'll go in ten days," said Okisko.

"Why ten days?" asked Ulalee.

"In ten days the moon will be but a thin sliver of pale light," explained Okisko. "That will be the best time to travel without being seen. We must be far away before anyone misses us."

For the next ten days, Ulalee and Okisko stopped walking by the sea at sunset. The fear in Lady Winona's heart eased. She thought her beloved wood thrush was at last learning patience. With this reassurance, Lady Winona slept soundly and failed to hear Ulalee the night she slipped from the house and ran to the edge of the forest to meet Okisko. It was a murky night. The stars were hidden, and the waning moon cast only a pale and sickly light.

When they were an hour from Croatoan, they stopped to rest under a giant water oak draped with long gray moss. For the first time since leaving, they spoke and laughed. But the laughter froze in their throats. For suddenly a silvery light burst all around them, blinding them for a moment. When they recovered their sight, they recoiled in horror. Old Cipo was standing before them. And they were surrounded by a ring of fire!

There was the medicine man, Cipo, shaking a rattle strung with alligator teeth at Ulalee and Okisko. The ring of fire crackled and spit, rising higher and higher.

Cipo called out, "Ulalee, come to me through the flames. I'll protect you. The flames will not harm you!"

"Never!" shouted Ulalee. "If I die, I'll die in Okisko's arms."

"Time is short!" warned Cipo. "Come now. The flames will not harm you!"

Okisko pulled Ulalee behind the giant oak, where Cipo could not see them. "Tell him to stop the flames and then you'll come out," whispered Okisko. "When the flames die down, you run away from Cipo. I'll put an arrow through his heart while his eyes are on you. Quickly, tell him to stop the fire!"

"Cipo, I'm afraid to come through the fire. I'll come if you stop the flames," called Ulalee from behind the tree.

Cipo shook his rattle and chanted magic words. The flames died down to a tiny smoldering circle.

Silently Okisko slipped an arrow from his quiver and fitted it to the bow.

Ulalee darted from the tree and ran with the wings of fear into the woods.

Cipo turned to follow her flight and lifted the rattle, shaking it in her direction.

Okisko took aim, then sent his arrow flying. The arrow struck Cipo's rattle, which exploded in a shower of fireballs. The fireballs flew in Ulalee's direction. Just as she leaped into the air over a fallen log, the fireballs struck her, and she fell behind the log.

Okisko was frozen, rooted to the spot. His arms and legs could not move, and his voice was gone.

Cipo dropped to his knees and chanted a long, wailing song in a language Okisko could not understand.

Gradually a light began to glow behind the log where Ulalee had fallen. It became brighter and brighter as Cipo's song grew louder. Before Okisko's eyes a shimmering white doe rose from behind the log. It stood for a moment, glowing in the dark night. Then it shook itself and bounded lightly off into the thick, dark woods.

Cipo's song ended, and he, too, vanished into the woods.

It was almost morning before Okisko could move his limbs again. Finally he staggered back to Croatoan and collapsed before Lady Winona's door.

Two Arrows

"*Ulalee!* Cipo! Ring of fire! A white doe!" babbled Okisko.

"What has happened? What are you saying, Okisko? Where is Ulalee?" asked Lady Winona.

But Okisko could only stammer a word or two that made no sense. Lady Winona gave him strong sassafras tea and made him rest. He fell into an exhausted sleep while she kept watch, fearing the worst for Ulalee.

When Okisko awakened, he told Lady Winona as best he could about the ring of fire. About Cipo's spell. About the shower of fireballs that struck Ulalee. About Cipo's magic song and Ulalee's reappearance as a white doe.

Lady Winona moaned and cried. "Oh, my beloved wood thrush! My wood thrush, what has Cipo done to you?"

"Is there no power greater than Cipo's?" asked Okisko.

Lady Winona abruptly stopped sobbing. "Yes. Yes,

there is. I know a medicine man who lives on the mainland. His name is Wenokan. He is said to be the most powerful of all."

"Will he help us?" asked Okisko.

"When I was a very young girl, Wenokan came to Croatoan. He was entertained by my father and took a great fancy to me. When he left, Wenokan told me that if ever I needed him, I had only to ask."

From her neck Lady Winona lifted a string that held one beautiful smoke-colored pearl. "Wenokan gave me this charm. 'Send it to me with any request,' he said when he took leave of us."

Okisko's eyes brightened with new hope.

"We have plans to make," whispered Lady Winona.

When Okisko recovered, he took Lady Winona's council and went to stay with friends on the mainland. At least, that was the message Lady Winona spread throughout Croatoan. Secretly the wise lady sent Okisko, with a message and her pearl charm, to the powerful medicine man.

Wenokan was moved by Okisko's woes and pleased that Lady Winona remembered him. He fashioned an arrow from an oyster shell. Then he took Okisko with him to a hidden fountain, the Magic Fountain of Roanoke.

"Thrust the arrow deep into the magic fountain," ordered Wenokan.

Okisko plunged the arrow into the water. It sizzled

and sparkled and sent forth a plume of hissing steam. He held firmly to the shaft of the arrow until the fountain was calm again. Then Okisko withdrew the arrow, amazed at what he saw.

"The oyster tip is changed. It gleams like polished mother-of-pearl!" he exclaimed.

Wenokan spoke. "With this arrow you must shoot the phantom doe."

"The doe is Ulalee. I could never shoot her!" cried Okisko.

"As the phantom doe dies, Ulalee will be reborn just the way she was before Cipo cast his spell," explained Wenokan.

Okisko knew he could trust Wenokan. He thanked the powerful man and rushed back to Croatoan with the magic arrow.

Lady Winona met Okisko at the edge of town. He could see that she was agitated.

"Okisko, thank the Great Spirit, you have come in time," she cried.

"I have come with good news," replied Okisko.

"Never mind. Later. You don't know what has happened in your absence."

"My news can wait. Tell me what so troubles you."

"The white doe has been sighted. Many have seen her at night. They say she is a bad omen for our village. A hunt has been organized for this very night. They'll kill my wood thrush!" moaned Lady Winona.

"Dry your tears and listen now to my news," said Okisko.

"There's something worse," cried Lady Winona. "Wanchese has joined the hunt. That evil man who has already killed so many of Ulalee's people is here in Croatoan."

"Have no fear of Wanchese," said Okisko.

"No fear! Are you mad? Wanchese is acknowledged the finest shot in the land. He's bragging that he will bring down the phantom doe with the silver arrow given to him by Queen Elizabeth."

Okisko finally calmed Lady Winona and with caution whispered into her ear all that had happened with the medicine man, Wenokan.

At twilight the men gathered for the hunt. When the last of the sun's rays were drowned in the vast ocean, the braves silently entered the forest. Okisko slipped away from the others. After a long hard run, he reached the giant water oak where he had last seen Ulalee in the form of the shining doe. He hid behind the tree and waited.

Soon a tiny speck of light appeared, moving through the dark woods. It grew brighter and larger as it came closer to the giant oak. Fifty cubits away Okisko could see the full shape of the phantom doe. His hand reached for the magic arrow. The doe came closer. Okisko's heart thumped wildly in his chest. He hesitated, fearing to kill his beloved Ulalee.

Then Wenokan's words ran through his head: She will be reborn just as she was. He laid the magic arrow against the taut bowstring and sent it flying straight to the heart of the gleaming doe.

But as Okisko's magic arrow flashed through the dark, another arrow also glinted in the starlight, streaking toward the phantom deer.

The doe rose on her hind legs and pawed the air with her front feet. She staggered and crashed to the ground. Okisko rushed to the mortally wounded deer. Two arrows had entered her heart, his mother-of-pearl arrow and a silver arrow of English make. Okisko heard the snap of a branch. He turned in time to glimpse Wanchese vanish into the blackness of the forest.

Okisko watched as the phantom doe changed into Ulalee, just as Wenokan had promised. She smiled at him. He bent his head to kiss her. Then her hand clutched the silver arrow that had pierced her heart. Her smile faded and her eyes closed. Ulalee was dead.

Okisko was so crazed he pulled the arrows from Ulalee and ran without stopping to the Magic Fountain of Roanoke. He plunged the arrows into the depths of the spring. The waters swallowed them with a fierce swirling movement, while Okisko screamed like a madman, "Bring her back! Bring her back!"

Okisko returned to the great water oak where he had left Ulalee. There he found nothing, neither doe nor

Ulalee. He sat under the tree all day and far into the night. Just before dawn he dozed, but was awakened by the sound of gentle pawing near his feet. Standing before him was the shining white doe. She looked at him for a moment with her beautiful wild violet eyes, then flicked her head lightly and bounded into the protective swamp.

Virginia Dare, Ulalee, white doe—life and spirit flowing in a never-ending stream. In the depths of the wild, mysterious Great Dismal Swamp she roams, a ghost deer. Many have sighted her, and some have been so bold as to try to capture the white doe. But none has succeeded and none ever shall.

Tom Lanning